This handbook belongs to:

_____

_____

_____

For Nancy and Janet

First edition 2015

Library of Congress Catalog Card Number 2014953086
ISBN 978-0-7636-7417-5

15 16 17 18 19 20 CCP 10 9 8 7 6 5 4 3 2 1
Printed in Shenzhen, Guangdong, China

This book was typeset in Joe.
The illustrations were done in acrylic.

Candlewick Press
99 Dover Street
Somerville, Massachusetts 02144

visit us at www.candlewick.com

Ragweed's
Farm Dog Handbook

Anne Vittur Kennedy

CANDLEWICK PRESS

I'm Ragweed. I'm a farm dog,
and I'm really, really good at it.
Most dogs aren't.

But don't worry. You'll be great.
You have the handbook.

Here's the first thing you need to know:
The rooster wakes the farmer early in the morning.

That's his job. That's not your job.
Don't wake the farmer.
You will really, really want to wake the farmer.
But don't wake the farmer.

If you DO wake the farmer,

Next, you need to know about pigs.
Pigs lie in the mud all day and get bigger and BIGGER.
That's their job. That's not your job.
Don't lie in the mud.

Mud is lovely.
It smells like worms and toes and earwax,
so you will really, really want to lie in the mud.
But don't lie in the mud.

If you DO lie in the mud, you will get a bath,
which is not lovely at all.

But you will get a biscuit after the bath.
So, OK then.

Now, about chickens.
Chickens sit on their nests and lay eggs.
That's their job. That's not your job.
Don't sit on their nests.

You will really, really want
to sit on their nests.
But don't sit on their nests.

If you DO sit on their nests,

Bonus advice:
Pretend you were chasing
a fox away and you will get
THREE biscuits!

(Give the fox one.)

Sheep grow curly hair,

which is used to make yarn

to knit sweaters for city dogs.

Sheep are fun to chase, too.
But that's not your job. Don't chase the sheep.

You will really, really want to chase the sheep.
But don't chase the sheep.

Exception:
If the farmer is away, chase the sheep!

Cows eat grass all day and make milk.

That's their job. That's not your job.
Don't eat grass.

You will really, really want to eat grass.
But don't eat grass.

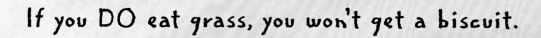

If you DO eat grass, you won't get a biscuit.

But you will throw up a biscuit,
and you can eat that one again.

So, that's how to be a good farm dog.
Let's review what you've learned:

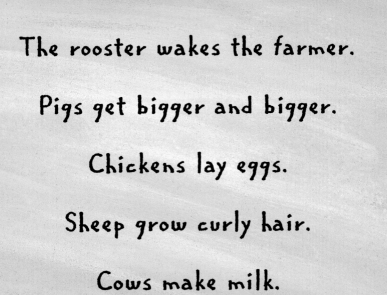

The rooster wakes the farmer.

Pigs get bigger and bigger.

Chickens lay eggs.

Sheep grow curly hair.

Cows make milk.

And what's the farm dog's job?

TO GET BISCUITS!

Now here's the best part. Watch this.
This is when I sit on the porch with the farmer.
He pats my head and tells me I'm a good farm dog.

Then I get a biscuit. Just for that!

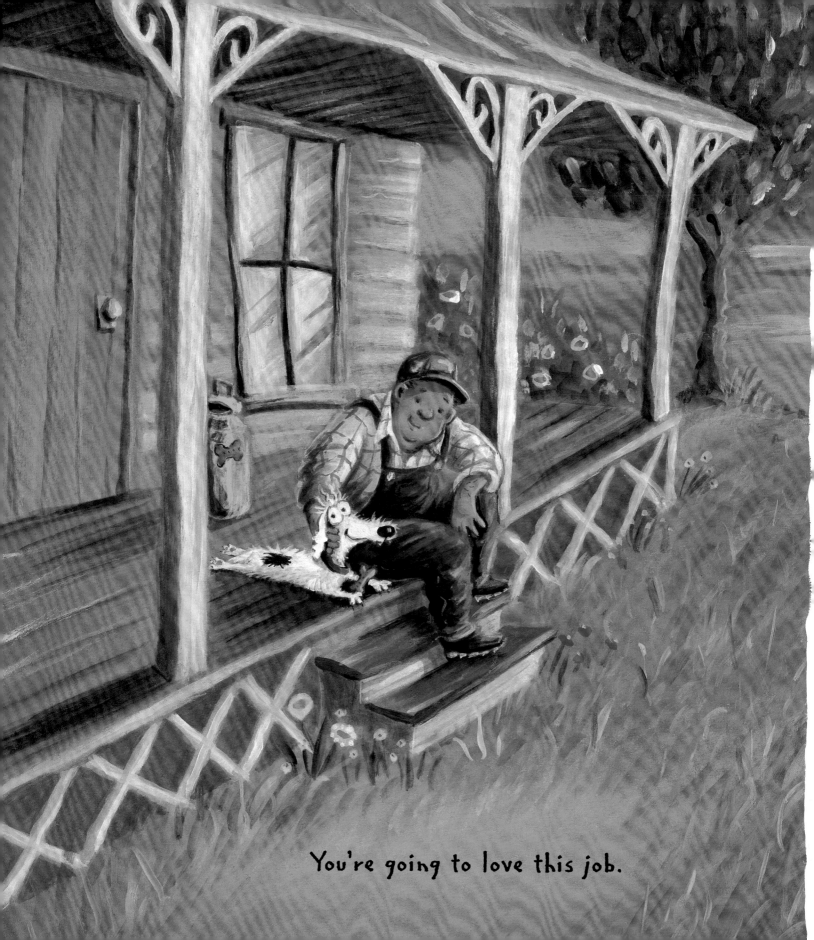

You're going to love this job.